THE
NOISY BOOK
TREASURY

MARGARET WISE BROWN

PICTURES BY LEONARD WEISGARD

DOVER PUBLICATIONS, INC.
MINEOLA, NEW YORK

Bibliographical Note

The Noisy Book Treasury, first published by Dover Publications, Inc., in 2014, is a republication of the following works: *The Noisy Book* (Harper & Row, Publishers, New York, 1939); *The Indoor Noisy Book* (HarperCollins Publishers, New York, 1994; originally published by Harper & Brothers Publishers, New York, 1942): and *The Quiet Noisy Book* (HarperCollins Publishers, New York, 1993; originally published by Harper & Brothers Publishers, New York, 1950).

International Standard Book Number

ISBN-13: 978-0-486-78028-3
ISBN-10: 0-486-78028-7

Manufactured in the United States by Courier Corporation
78028701   2014
www.doverpublications.com

CONTENTS

THE
NOISY BOOK
TREASURY

NOISY

BOOK

One day a little dog named Muffin got a cinder in his eye. Poor little Muffin. His eye hurt him. It stung. So they took him to the dog doctor.

The dog doctor said, «Muffin, I will put this bandage over your eyes and when you take it off tonight your eye won't hurt you any more.»

And there was Muffin with a great big white bandage over his eyes.

**Everything looked as dark to him
as when you close your eyes**

BUT

MUFFIN COULD HEAR

Muffin pricked up his ears

he heard everything in the
room that made a noise

he heard

TICK TOCK TICK TOCK

(it was the clock)

he heard

SISSS SISSSSSSS

(it was the radiator)

he heard

SNIP SNAP SNIP SNAP

(it was a pair of scissors)

he heard

TING A LING A LING

(it was the telephone)

he heard

GRRRRRR GRRRRRRR

(it was his own stomach growling)

he heard

BZZZ BZZZzzzzzzz

(it was a little black fly)

he heard

KERCHOOO

(it was the dog doctor sneezing)

Then Muffin went down the
street on his way home.
«Poor little Muffin,» said the
people on the street.
«Muffin has a big white bandage over his eyes and he can't
see a thing.»

But
Muffin could hear.

Muffin pricked up his
ears and heard all the
noises on the street.

First he heard the big noises

MEN HAMMERING

Bang bang bang

AUTOMOBILE HORNS

Awuurra awuurra

HORSES HOOFS

Clop clop Clop clop

ANOTHER LITTLE DOG

Bow wow wow

Then he heard the biggest noise on the street

**Then the sun began to shine
Could Muffin hear that?**

Then he heard the little noises

Bzzzzzz bzzzzzz
a bee
Swishhhh swishhh
car wheels
Chirp chirp
a bird
Meoww meoww
a pussycat
Patter patter patter patter
people's feet
Flippity flap flap flap
an awning in the wind

It began to snow
But could Muffin hear that?

Then he heard a little noise

and he didn't know what it was

squeak

squeak

squeak

It was not a mouse

What could it be?

Was it

a big horse going squeak squeak squeak?

NO

Was it

a policeman going squeak squeak squeak?

NO

Was it

a garbage can?

NO

Was it

a big fierce lion?

NO

Was it

an empty house?

NO

Was it

an engine and a coal car?

NO

Was it

a big boat?

NO

Was it

an airplane?

NO

What do **YOU** think it was?

It was a **BABY DOLL**

**And they gave the baby doll
to Muffin for his very own.**

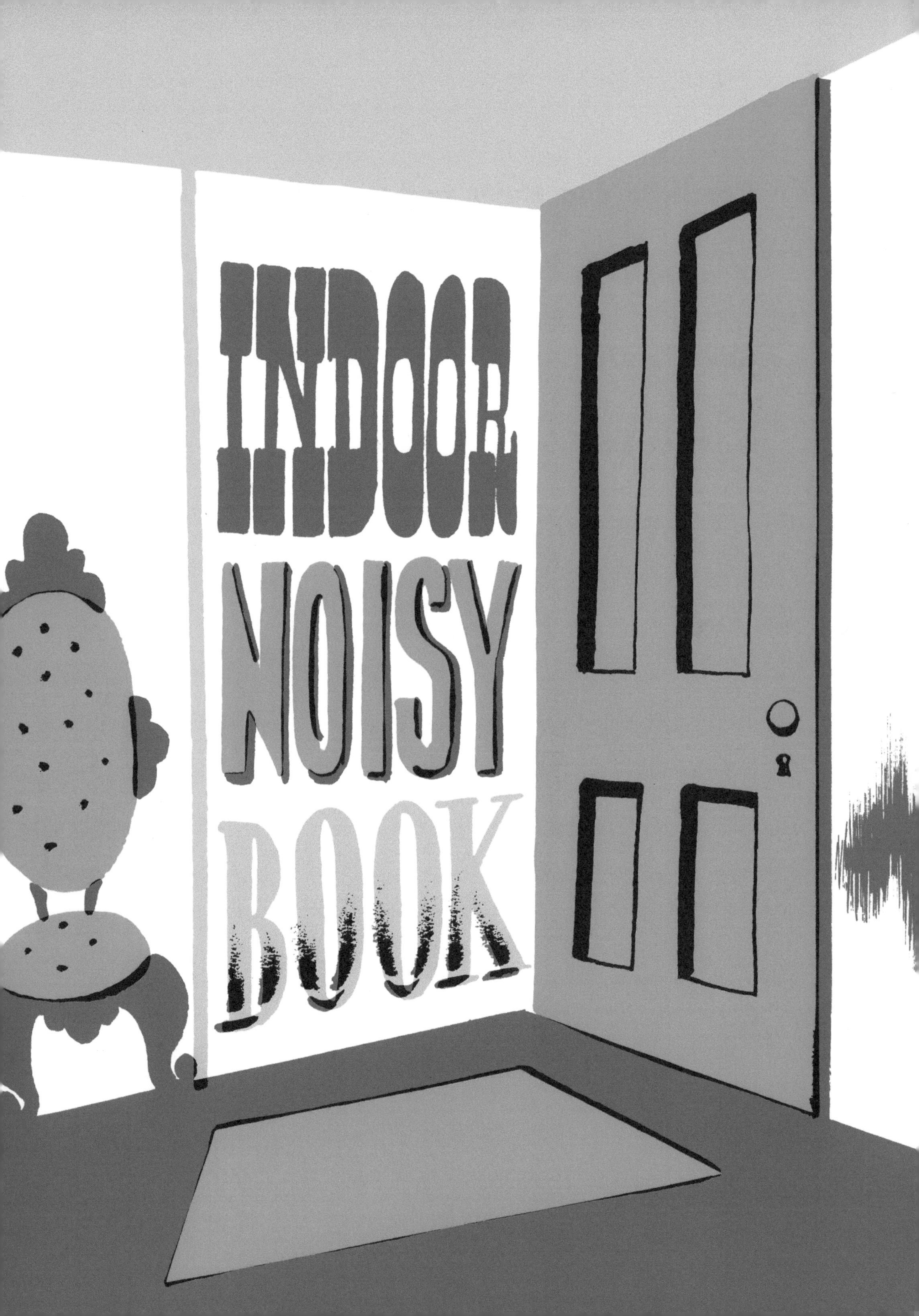
INDOOR
NOISY
BOOK

The little dog Muffin had a cold.

You can't go outdoors Muffin, they said. You

have to stay in the house all day and sleep

a lot in your own little bed.

So what could Muffin do?

He curled up in his bed

and closed his eyes

and cocked his ears

and there he was.

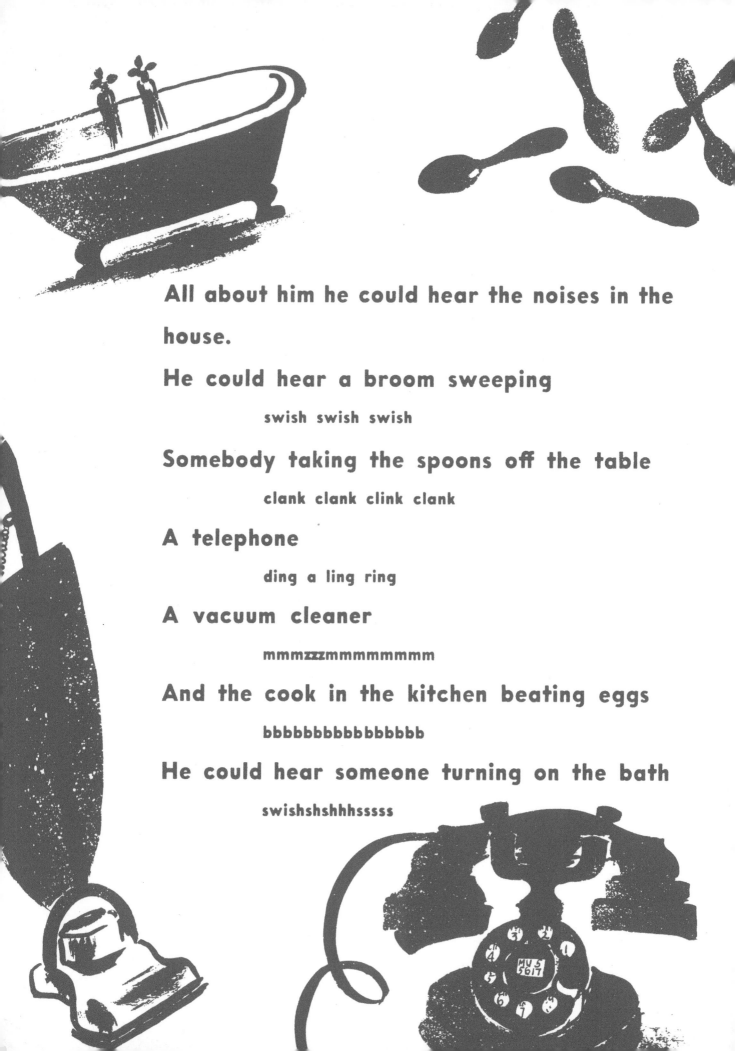

All about him he could hear the noises in the house.

He could hear a broom sweeping

swish swish swish

Somebody taking the spoons off the table

clank clank clink clank

A telephone

ding a ling ring

A vacuum cleaner

mmmzzzmmmmmmmm

And the cook in the kitchen beating eggs

bbbbbbbbbbbbbbbb

He could hear someone turning on the bath

swishshshhhsssss

Then Muffin heard someone dropping a pin.

Or could he hear that?

And he heard a fly buzzing

      How was that?

And he heard a wasp

      How was that!

And someone slammed the front door

      How was that?

Someone else was reading a book

      But could Muffin hear that?

And then there was a rattle of dishes. That meant lunch.

What kind of a noise did lunch make?

They had celery for lunch
Could Muffin hear that?

And soup
Could Muffin hear that?

And raw carrots
and steak
and spinach
Could Muffin hear that?

And some very quiet custard for dessert

Outside it began to rain.

Then the rain turned to snow.

Then the snow turned to hail and sleet

hssssssss   ping ping ping

Everything got white outside.

In the room everything got grey.

Muffin could hear the wind

whoo whoo whoo

And the sleet and snow

And the cars on the snowy road

How was that?

It began to get dark.

And all over the town the lights turned on
all at once.

   But could Muffin hear that?

   NO

But Muffin did hear them turn on the light
in his own room
        click

And then all around him was warm electric
light.

And he could hear everyone coming up the
stairs to see the little dog who had a cold.

First he could hear the little boy's feet
coming up the stairs
        How was that?
    pat pat pat pat

Then he could hear the little boy's mother's footsteps

How was that?

patter patter patter

Then the little boy's father's footsteps

How was that?

clump clump clump

Then the cook's footsteps

How was that?

Dump Dump-de-dumma-de Dump

Then he heard some little tiny footsteps coming to see him.

Muffin could just hear them coming softly up the stairs.

Was it a little bug coming to see Muffin?

NO

Was it an elephant coming to see Muffin?

NO

Was it a soldier?

NO

Was it a sailor?

NO

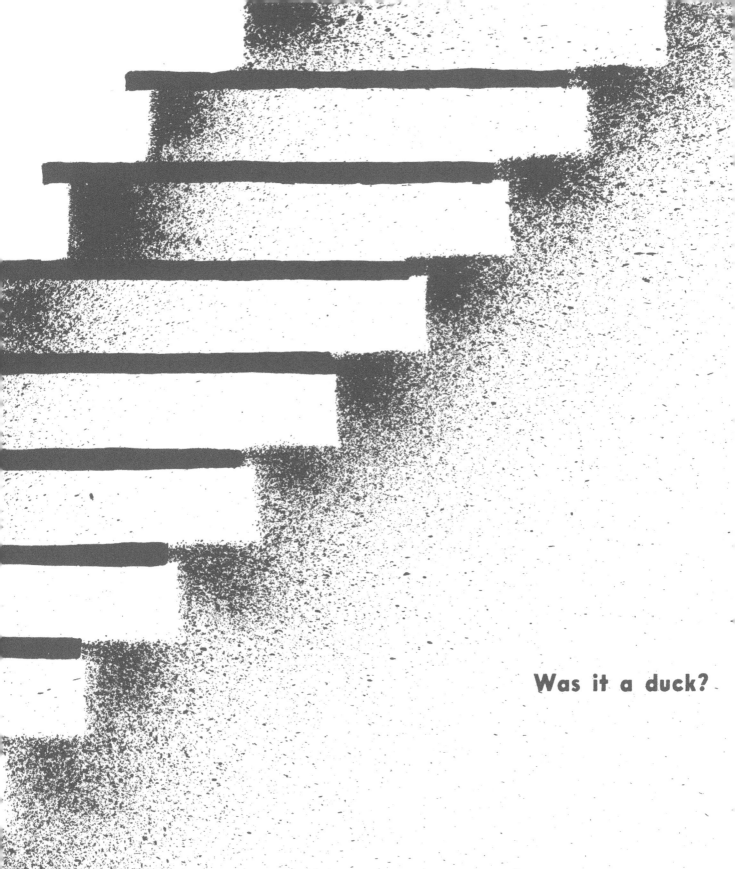

Was it a duck?

NO

Was it a clown with a firecracker?

NO

Was it a whiskered mouse?

NO

What could it be?

It was the cat, of course.

And the cat came right into the room.

Everyone brought Muffin a present.

And the cook brought him his dinner and

they all watched him eat it.

The next day Muffin didn't have a cold any more and he went outdoors again and listened to the birds and the trucks.

THE

QUIET
NOISY

OK

Muffin, the little dog who heard everything, had been asleep all night. Quietly something woke him up. A very quiet noise. What could it be?

Was it an ant crawling?

Was it a bee wondering?

Was it an

ELEPHANT

tiptoeing

down

stairs?

NO

Was it a

little blue flower

growing?

NO

WAS
IT
A
SKYSCRAPER
SCRAPING
THE
SKY?

NO

Was it a cow

putting on

her petticoat?

WAS IT

A GRASSHOPPER

SNEEZING?

NO

Was
it
a
mouse

SIGHING?

WAS

IT

A FISH

BREATHING?

NO

It was a very quiet noise.

Such a quiet noise.

As quiet as quietness.

It was a very quiet noise.

AS QUIET AS SOMEONE
EATING CURRANT JELLY.

AS QUIET AS A LITTLE KITTEN
LAPPING MILK.

QUIET AS A BIRD'S WING
CUTTING THE AIR.

QUIET AS SNOW FALLING.

QUIET AS A CHAIR.

QUIET AS AIR.

QUIET AS SOMEONE WHISPERING A SECRET TO A BABY.

What do you think it was?

Muffin knew what it was!

It was—

the sun

coming up

It was the morning breeze.

It was the birds turning over in their nests.

It was the rooster opening his mouth to crow.

It was the day.

It was a wheel turning halfway round.

It was an alarm clock springing to ring.

It was a butterfly unfolding his wings.

It was the milkman whispering to his horse.

It was a new leaf uncurling.

It was the flies opening their million-cornered eyes.

It was all the flowers blooming on that day.

It was the sound of an early bird catching a worm.

It was the sound of the dew rising up to the sun.

It was a balloon about to pop.

It was a man about to think.

It was a slow fig ripening.

IT WAS
THE
NEW DAY